MW00951530

Skippy ChipMunk The Artist

ISBN 978-0-9977134-3-5

Skippy ChipMunk The Artist

by Susan Scarince Jones

There were many things Skippy ChipMunk liked to do.

He liked to play with his trains.

He liked to play with his dirt bike.

He liked to play with his blocks.

He even liked to read a good book now and then.

Can you guess what
Skippy liked to do
the best?

He loved to paint!

He painted all the
beautiful things he saw
in his garden.

In the winter when the garden was covered with snow, Skippy had his colorful paintings on his walls. They were a reminder that summer would always return.

One day, Skippy decided he would like to paint a portrait.
A portrait is a painting of someone.

"Who could I paint?" he wondered.
"May I paint your portrait?" he asked the garden gnome.
"Not today," said the gnome. "I must watch over the garden.
The rabbits are eating my daisies."

Just then, Skippy saw the shy little yellow flower fairy.
She ran away before he could ask to paint her portrait.

"May I paint your portrait, Mr. Toad?" asked Skippy.
"I don't have the time!" said Mr. Toad with a frown.

Mr. Squirrel was sitting on the nearby fence.
"Would you like me to paint your portrait?" asked Skippy.
"I'm too busy collecting food for the winter," said the squirrel
as he scampered away.

Skippy was about to give up hope.
Suddenly, he heard a noise among the ferns.
It was Lavender the flower fairy.
"What are you doing, Skippy?" she asked.
"I'm looking for someone who would like to have their portrait
painted, but everyone is too shy or busy," he said sadly.

"Well, I'm not too busy today," said Lavender.
"Hooray!" shouted Skippy.
"If you'll sit right down here we can get started," he said.

Lavender sat down while Skippy got his paints and brushes ready. He told her he would need red, yellow, blue, green and white paint.

"You'll have to try to sit very, very still," Skippy told Lavender as he began to paint. "I will try my best," she said.

Skippy painted all morning long.
He was having so much fun, he lost track of time!
Finally, they both agreed it was time to take a little break.
"May I please see my painting now?" asked Lavender.
"Not yet," replied Skippy. "I want it to be a surprise!"

After they had a snack and stretched a bit,
they went back to the painting.
Skippy only had a little more to do.
Finally, he stepped away from the painting and smiled.

"TA-DA, It's all finished!" he shouted.

"Now you can take a look. I hope you like it,"
said Skippy ChipMunk shyly.

When Lavender saw it, her eyes opened wide.
"It's beautiful!" she sighed. "It looks just like me."

Before they knew it, everyone who lived in the garden gathered around the painting. Even grumpy Mr. Toad said he liked the painting.
Now they ALL wanted to
have their portraits painted!

Skippy thought for a moment.
"I have an idea," he exclaimed.
"Painting is so much fun and makes me feel happy.
I would like to teach you how to paint," he said.
"Well, I don't think I could ever paint like you do,"
said the garden gnome.
"Me neither," said the others, shaking their heads.
"But you can try! It just takes a little practice.
Tomorrow let's all meet at my art studio," said Skippy.

Every day they all gathered at Skippy ChipMunk's art studio.
He was a very good teacher. By the end of the summer,
everyone learned how to paint. They were delighted by
the beautiful artwork they could now create.

Skippy decided it was time for them to have an art show.
Proudly, they set their art work up in the garden so everyone could see their beautiful paintings.
They served cookies and punch to all who stopped by.
The garden was buzzing with excitement!

Soon winter came and the garden was covered with snow.
It was very cold and quiet outside.

Inside, everyone had their bright and colorful paintings
on their walls. It was a happy reminder
that spring and summer *would always return.*

Before long,
spring and
summer
did return!

And thanks to Skippy ChipMunk, everyone
kept right on painting!

This book is dedicated to my wonderful
husband Alan. Thank you so much for all your
encouragement and support. Oh, and for all those bags of bird seed for Skippy!
A special thank you also to my daughter Kristen and to my granddaughter Aly.

Skippy ChipMunk is a real live chipmunk who lives in my backyard
in Northern New Jersey. All the photos of him are real and not photoshopped.
I love taking photos of nature and doing artwork of all kinds.

Be sure to look for my other Skippy ChipMunk books:

Skippy ChipMunk Where are you going?
Skippy ChipMunk's Birthday Surprise!

www.skippychipmunk.com
susimage66@gmail.com

Made in the USA
Middletown, DE
14 February 2019